Fanny the Champ

by Nalini Raghunandan

To Josa Emiliz and Jozeff Ellie Dela Cruz

Dream big

Nalini Raghunandan

May /13/ 2017

Tellwell Talent
www.tellwell.ca

ISBN
978-1-77302-327-4 (Hardcover)
978-1-77302-328-1 (Paperback)

Dedicated

To my daughters Dianne and Shivon

Oh, what a beautiful sunny day! Fanny
walks happily along the seashore, barking
good morning to all the villagers passing by.

Fanny is a beautiful dog with shiny
brown hair and spots of white.

Fanny greets Rachael, the local school teacher, with a hearty
bark. WOOF! "Good morning, Fanny!" Rachael replies.

Next, he spies Pinky, the local dentist, and greets her with a lick on her hand.
SLURP! "Nice to see you, Fanny", Pinky says, scratching him behind the ear.

Finally, he spots Hasani, the village butcher, and greets him
with a playful growl. GRRR! "Have a super day Fanny", says
Hasani, laughing out loud.

Fanny always enjoys looking at the fishermen and fisherwomen as they bring in their boats loaded with their catches from the previous night.

The fishermen and fisherwomen
set up a market every morning.
The villagers buy fresh fish every day.

They all know Fanny very well and adore him very much,
especially Miss Leela, Bill, and particularly Mr. Ed,
who treats Fanny like a member of the family.

That's because a long time ago, Mr. Ed found Fanny at the side of the road, scared, tiny, and hungry. He was just a puppy.

Mr. Ed fed him some biscuits he had in his pocket, and took him home.

He named him Fanny. Since that day, Fanny has lived with Mr. Ed, his wife, and his two small children.

Every morning, Fanny waits for Mr. Ed by the shore until he gets back from his night-time fishing trip. Mr. Ed greets Fanny by scratching his head and rubbing his back. Fanny responds by licking Mr. Ed's face and wagging his tail most happily.

"How is my Fanny?", Mr. Ed asks excitedly. Fanny gives two cheery barks and a howl in reply:
"WOOF! WOOF! AWOO!"

The fishermen always throw him a fish. One particular day, Bill said, "Here boy, I have something special for you." Bill gave him a bigger-than-usual fish; he gave him a juicy catfish, with big whiskers.

"Fanny", Miss Leela said, "This is for you. A shrimp got caught in my fishing net last night." Miss Leela peeled the shrimp before she gave it to Fanny.

Fanny took his fish and shrimp under the mango tree to enjoy his meal.

After eating, Fanny always goes for a swim. Fanny is an excellent swimmer.

The villagers were being very loud, bargaining with the fishermen and fisherwomen. Tuma, who is 4 years old, came to the market with his mom.

He slipped from her hand as he was playing with his red and white ball. The ball rolled to the edge of the shore. Tuma hurried after it!

Fanny spotted him and sensed
danger. He barked and barked,
and even howled "AOOOOO!",
but no one heard him.

While trying to reach his ball, Tuma had fallen into the water, and the tide had washed him away from the shore.

Quick as lightning, Fanny ran to the shore
and plunged into the water. He swam out to
Tuma and grabbed him by his shirt collar.

Tuma's mom, suddenly realizing he wasn't next to her, panicked and shouted, "Tuma! Tuma! Has anyone seen my Tuma?!" The crowd became alarmed.

Mr. Ed finally saw them and everyone ran to the shore. They got there just in time to see a heroic Fanny holding onto Tuma as he swam him to safety.

Tuma was frightened but out of danger, and he hugged Fanny in thanks. Relieved, Tuma's mom lifted him up and hugged him tightly.

The villagers, and especially Tuma's mother, patted and hugged Fanny in thanks. They dried him with a blue towel.

From that day on, he was known as Fanny the Champ.

CPSIA information can be obtained
at www.ICGtesting.com
Printed in the USA
LVOW06*0343250417
532090LV00010B/32/P